Dear Parent:

Congratulations! Your child is taking the first steps on an exciting journey. The destination? Independent reading!

STEP INTO READING® will help your child get there. The program offers five steps to reading success. Each step includes fun stories and colorful art. There are also Step into Reading Sticker Books, Step into Reading Math Readers, Step into Reading Phonics Readers, Step into Reading Write-In Readers, and Step into Reading Phonics Boxed Sets—a complete literacy program with something to interest every child.

Learning to Read, Step by Step!

Ready to Read   Preschool–Kindergarten
• big type and easy words • rhyme and rhythm • picture clues
For children who know the alphabet and are eager to begin reading.

Reading with Help   Preschool–Grade 1
• basic vocabulary • short sentences • simple stories
For children who recognize familiar words and sound out new words with help.

Reading on Your Own   Grades 1–3
• engaging characters • easy-to-follow plots • popular topics
For children who are ready to read on their own.

Reading Paragraphs   Grades 2–3
• challenging vocabulary • short paragraphs • exciting stories
For newly independent readers who read simple sentences with confidence.

Ready for Chapters   Grades 2–4
• chapters • longer paragraphs • full-color art
For children who want to take the plunge into chapter books but still like colorful pictures.

STEP INTO READING® is designed to give every child a successful reading experience. The grade levels are only guides. Children can progress through the steps at their own speed, developing confidence in their reading, no matter what their grade.

Remember, a lifetime love of reading starts with a single step!

For Laura and Peter with love!
—A.S.C.

For my future child and my family,
who have prayed for me
—A.P.

Text copyright © 2012 by Alyssa Satin Capucilli
Cover art and interior illustrations copyright © 2012 by Ariel Pang

Published in the United States by Random House Children's Books, a division of Random House, Inc.,
New York.

Step into Reading, Random House, and the Random House colophon are registered trademarks of
Random House, Inc.

Visit us on the Web!
StepIntoReading.com
randomhouse.com/kids

Educators and librarians, for a variety of teaching tools, visit us at randomhouse.com/teachers

Library of Congress Cataloging-in-Publication Data
Capucilli, Alyssa Satin.
Monkey play / by Alyssa Satin Capucilli ; illustrated by Ariel Pang.
  p. cm. — (Step into reading. Step 1)
Summary: Three little monkeys swing through a market in India causing mayhem as they playfully
pass through the stalls.
ISBN 978-0-375-86993-8 (pbk.) — ISBN 978-0-375-96993-5 (lib. bdg.) — ISBN 978-0-375-98626-0 (ebook)
[1. Stories in rhyme. 2. Monkeys—Fiction. 3. Markets—Fiction. 4. India—Fiction.]
I. Pang, Ariel, ill. II. Title.
PZ8.3.C1935 Mon 2012 [E]—dc23 2011044499

Printed in the United States of America

10 9 8 7 6 5 4 3 2 1

Monkey Play

by Alyssa Satin Capucilli

illustrated by Ariel Pang

Random House 🏠 New York

Way up high,
in a big palm tree,
sits one little monkey.

Then two.

Then three!

Monkeys jump.

Monkeys play.

Look!
More monkeys
on the way!

9

Little monkeys
love to swing.

Little monkeys
love to sing.

Monkeys love
to climb up far.

Monkeys on rugs
and a big spice jar!

Monkeys hold on
with their tails.

Monkeys bounce
on silky sails.

Monkeys leap.

Monkeys slide.

By fruits and flowers, monkeys hide!

Monkeys love
to dress up, too,
in shiny hats
and sparkly shoes!

Monkeys nibble,
and monkeys take
banana pie!
A coconut shake!

23

Monkeys roll.
Monkeys run,
under the moon
or the setting sun.

Monkeys sneak
into a tent so tall,
with elephants
and camels.
There's room for all!

More monkeys come.

And others, too.

Cows, goats, parrots,

and the royal zoo!

Monkeys <u>love</u>
to play with friends.

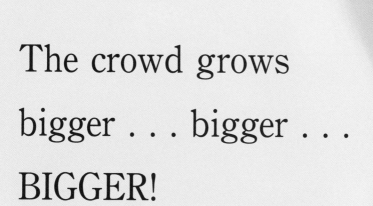

The crowd grows
bigger . . . bigger . . .
BIGGER!

31

Monkeys hope
it never ends!